Be Safe. ♥

Written and Illustrated by
Russell Habermann

Paul has a problem.

Mama Bunyan is always worried about Paul's safety and doesn't let him have any fun.

Every time he goes biking,
she makes him use a helmet.

Every time he goes swimming,
she makes him use a life jacket.

And every time they go driving,
she makes him use a booster seat.

Paul thinks using a helmet and a life jacket
and a booster seat is <u>not</u> fun.

Mama Bunyan always says the same thing:
"Better safe than sorry!"

But Paul doesn't want to be safe.

Paul wants to have freedom.
Paul wants to have adventure.

Paul wants to have fun!

One day, Mama Bunyan asks, "What
do you want to do today?"

Paul says, "Nothing! Because you would make me use a helmet or a life jacket or some other silly thing."

Mama Bunyan says, "But you know why I make you use things like a helmet and a life jacket, right?"

Paul answers, "Because you're afraid."

Mama Bunyan says, "Well, the world is a dangerous place. And I am afraid you could get hurt.

"But the real reason is because
I want you to have fun.

"I want you to go biking and swimming and skating and skiing and snowboarding.

"I want you to have all the fun. And I want you to be safe so you can <u>keep</u> having fun."

Then she says, "And do you know why
I want you to keep having fun?"

Paul asks, "Why?"

And Mama Bunyan says, "Because I love you."

The End. ♥

Made in the USA
Monee, IL
03 September 2021